SnOring Beauty

WRITTEN BY
BRUCE HALE

ILLUSTRATED BY
HOWARD FINE

HARCOURT, INC. Orlando Austin New York San Diego London

Blexus

Fleabitis

Tintinnitus

Beebo

Nostrilene

Umpudine

HeXus

www.HarcourtBooks.com

Library of Congress Cataloging-in-Publication Data
Hale, Bruce.
Snoring Beauty/Bruce Hale; illustrated by Howard Fine.
p. cm.
Summary: An adaptation of the traditional tale, featuring a sleeping,
snoring princess who is rescued by a prince after being cursed by a bad fairy.
[1. Fairy tales.   2. Folklore—Germany.] I. Fine, Howard, 1961–, ill.
II. Sleeping Beauty. English. III. Title.
PZ8.H132Sno 2008
398.2—dc22
[E]   2006022950
ISBN 978-0-15-216314-3

C E G H F D B

Manufactured in China

The illustrations in this book were done in watercolors.
The display type was created by Monica Dengo.
The text type was set in Fifteen36.
Color separations by Colourscan Co. Pte. Ltd., Singapore
Manufactured by South China Printing Company, Ltd., China
Production supervision by Christine Witnik
Designed by April Ward

To *Janette, my sweet inspiration*
—B. H.

For my sleeping beauties—
Rona, Elana, and Emma
—H. F.

Fred

LONG, LONG AGO (about six hundred and two years ago last Friday, at 7:00 P.M., Fairy Standard Time, to be exact), the childless King Gluteus and his wife, Queen Esophagus, got lucky at last.

"A baby girl!" Queen Esophagus cried.

"I'll eat to that!" said King Gluteus.

For the rest of us—peasants and milkmaids and frogs—it was business as usual.

Yada yada, hippity-hop.

The king and queen threw a big wingding for their daughter's christening. They invited every fairy from far and wide. But, wouldn't you know it, they left one out: this really cranky fairy named Beebo, who was off hosting a garlic festival.

On christening day, the baby girl was named Princess Drachmina Lofresca Malvolio Margarine. Poor little tadpole. She smiled and cooed, anyway.

The dining hall bulged with lords and ladies. And up at the main table with the king and queen sat seven of the funkiest fairies you've ever seen: Hexus and Blexus, Nostrilene and Umpudine, Fleabitis and Tintinnitus, and Fred (who wasn't really a fairy, but no one had the heart to tell him).

ust as they began a round of rude
ry songs, the king clapped his hands.
ime to bless the baby!"

Eh?" said Tintinnitus, who was
lf-deaf. "Slime with flesh and
avy? No thanks. I'll be back in
twinkle."

And she waddled off.

One by one, fairies shuffled past to bless Princess Drachmina Lofresca Malvolio Margarine (Marge for short).

"She will be the most beauteous maiden in the land," said Hexus.

"She will be the wittiest," said Blexus.

And on and on: best dancer blah-blah-blah, best singer blah-blah-blah, nicest penmanship blah-blah-blah…

Yada yada, hippity-hop.

Until…

BAM! The door blew open.

There stood Beebo the fairy. She looked like trouble,
and she smelled like garlic.

"So sorry I'm late," she snarled sweetly. "The carrier pigeon
must have EATEN MY INVITATION!"

She stuck her big bazoo into the crib and barked, "When this babe turns sixteen, she will be run over by a pie wagon and die!"

Tintinnitus returned just at that moment. "Eh, what's that?" she said. "She'll turn into a dragon and fly?"

"Die!" snapped Beebo.

"Spy?" asked Tintinnitus.

"DIE!" shouted the Garlicky One.

"Oh, my," said Tintinnitus.

With a grumble and a growl, Beebo blasted off.

Tintinnitus turned to King Gluteus and Queen Esophagus.
She could not undo Beebo's gift. But she could bamboozle it.
   "My blessing is that, um…instead of turning into a dead dragon—"
   "But Beebo said—" the king began.
   "Your daughter will become…a *sleeping* dragon!" Tintinnitus
continued. "And one day, she'll be awakened by…uh…um…"
   "A prince?" said the queen hopefully.
   "A quince," said the fairy. "Good idea."
   And, *foof*, she was gone.

First thing the next day, King Gluteus
banned all pie wagons from the kingdom.
In fact, he banned all pies—even mud pies.
"That should stop the curse,"
said the king.
"Let them eat cake!" sang
Queen Esophagus.

Y EARS HOPPED ALONG like a toad with
arthritis. Princess Marge blossomed and grew.
And as she grew, she became kind and beautiful,
sweet and clever.

As the fairies promised, Marge could sing like a
nightingale, dance like sunlight on the water, sew
a wedding dress blindfolded, make a chocolate cake
from dirt and rocks, build a house in a single day....

Yada yada, hippity-hop.

The fairies forgot just one thing:
She was too perfect. Nobody wanted to
play with a girl who could do everything
twice as well as they could.

Princess Marge was lonely.

The day the princess turned sixteen, an old woman in a wagon rolled up to the castle. "Let me in," she pleaded. "I bring a yummy-nummy treat for the princess."

The young guard spied a wagonload of pastries round as wheels. A sweet smell made his belly rumble. *Yummy-nummy,* indeed! After so many years, he didn't know a pie from a pollywog.

The guard opened the gates.

The wagon trundled inside.

At that very moment—what are the odds, I ask you?—Marge was crossing the road to the cake shop. The street was steep, the wagon wobbled, and before you knew it, the pie wagon swerved and crunched over her foot.

"Yow!" cried Princess Marge. And just as Tintinnitus foretold...

ALLA-BAM!

Marge turned into a dragon, and…

ALLA-BEEP!

She fell deeply asleep.

Now, legend says that the whole
castle conked out, too.

Yeah, right.

Here's what really happened: The
sleeping dragon princess began to snore.

SquOnnnnk-sheeeOoo!
SquOnnnnk-sheeeOoo!

And besides being the fanciest dancer
and best cake baker in the kingdom,
Princess Marge was—naturally—the loudest
snoring dragon.

SquOnnnnk-sheeeOoo!
SquOnnnnk-sheeeOoo!

Did everyone rush to congratulate Marge
on her perfect snores? They did not. No one
comforted her enchanted sleep. The dragon
princess dreamed lonely dreams.

Days passed. No one could sleep with the racket and ruckus. Those with carriages visited far-off kingdoms. Those without wore earplugs and shouted. The king did what kings always do. He made a proclamation.

KING GLUTEUS WANTS YOU

to break the curse and awaken his sleeping daughter with a quince. (Use of quince to be determined by applicant.)

REWARD: Half the kingdom, the princess's hand in marriage, and a set of elf-made garden furniture.

Employees of castle not eligible.
If princess awakens but remains a dragon, tough luck—you still have to marry her.
Offer not valid in the kingdoms of Smorg, Spiffle, and Quog. Void where prohibited.

Men came to test their luck. With brass and
bluster and bright ideas, they tried to awaken the
dragon princess.

One spooned quince curry between her lips.
Marge snored on.

One tickled her with the leaves of a quince tree.
SquO-ha-ha-honk, shee-hee-hee-Ooo!
SquO-ha-ha-honk, shee-hee-hee-Ooo!
Marge snored on.

One pelted her with ripe quinces.
Close, but no cigar.
Marge snored on.

Months passed.
Suitors came, and suitors went.
They sang quince songs and baked quince pies, they told quince jokes and sighed quince sighs. They built a quince alarm clock that squirted jam and jelly. They made a quince-filled rubber ball to bounce upon her belly.

But nothing worked.
Yada yada, hippity-hop.
Marge snored on.

Then one day, a dusty young man clip-clopped into town. "What's that awful noise?" he asked a milkmaid.

"WHAT?" she shouted. "I CAN'T HEAR YOU! I AM WEARING EARPLUGS!"

She took them out.

"I SAID, WHAT'S THAT NOISE?" bellowed the man.

"No need to shout!" said the milkmaid. And she told him Marge's sad, sad story.

The man studied the dragon princess.
She was pretty cute—for a dragon.
He timed her snores.

SqUOnnnnk-sheeeOoo!

He leaned into the blast, ears ringing.

SquOnnnnk-sheeeOoo!

His hair blew back, but he puckered up.

SquOnnnnk-sheeeOoo!

Then...

Smack!
Blink!
Those dragon eyes popped open, and—
yada yada, hippity-hop—
Marge's scales melted, her tail shriveled,
and she shrank...

back into a human girl again.

"Are you a wizard?" she asked the man.

"Golly, no, I'm a prince," he said.

"Prince Quince, to be exact."

Well, the king kept his word. And in two shakes of a frog's flipper, the prince and princess got hitched. This time, *all* the fairies in the land were invited.

The kingdom whooped it up with a *hey-nonny-nonny* and a *hot-cha-cha*.

"Do you love me?" asked the princess.

"With all my heart," said the prince.

"Even though I'm the best at everything?"

Prince Quince smiled. "Honey, nobody's perfect."

At last the newlyweds tiptoed off to their chambers, where they whispered sweet nothings and drifted to sleep.

Later that night, something awakened the prince.
Squonnnnk-sheeeOoo!
Squonnnnk-sheeeOoo!
Prince Quince sighed. He kissed his wife's cheek,
stuffed some earplugs into his ears, and rolled over.

And, despite the truly royal ruckus...

they lived happily—and *noisily*—ever after.